Reading Together at Home

"Have you Seen the Crocodile?"

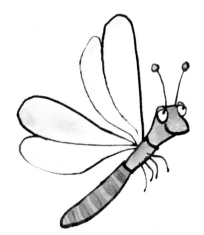

First U.S. edition 1998

ISBN 0-7636-0533-6

2 4 6 8 10 9 7 5 3 1

Printed in Hong Kong

Candlewick Press
2067 Massachusetts Avenue
Cambridge, Massachusetts 02140

"Have you Seen the Crocodile?"

Colin West

DISCOVERY TOYS CANDLEWICK PRESS

"Have you seen the crocodile?"
asked the parrot.

"No,"
said the
dragonfly.

"Have you seen the crocodile?"
asked the parrot
and the dragonfly.

"No,"
said the
bumblebee.

"Have you seen the crocodile?"
asked the parrot
and the dragonfly
and the bumblebee.

"No,"
said the
butterfly.

"Have you seen the crocodile?"
asked the parrot
and the dragonfly
and the bumblebee
and the butterfly.

"No,"
said the
hummingbird.

"Have you seen the crocodile?"
asked the parrot
and the dragonfly
and the bumblebee
and the butterfly
and the hummingbird.

"No," said the frog.

"No one's seen the crocodile!"
said the parrot
and the dragonfly
and the bumblebee
and the butterfly
and the hummingbird
and the frog.

But then . . .

"I'VE SEEN THE CROCODILE!"
snapped the crocodile.

"Have YOU seen the parrot
and the dragonfly
and the bumblebee
and the butterfly
and the hummingbird
and the frog?"

asked the crocodile.

Read it again

Words and pictures

Combining words and pictures can be an enjoyable way to help children read the words. Your child can try reading the end of the story like this.

"No one's seen the ![crocodile]!" said the ![parrot]

and the ![dragonfly] and the ![bee] and the ![butterfly]

and the ![hummingbird] and the ![frog]. But then . . .

"I'VE SEEN THE ![crocodile]!" snapped the ![crocodile]

"Have YOU seen the ![parrot] and the ![dragonfly] and the ![bee]

and the ![butterfly] and the ![hummingbird] and the ![frog]?"

asked the

Act it out

The pattern of the story makes it easy for children to act it out themselves or with toys. They could use different voices for the animals and add sound effects.

Animal alphabet

Children can complete lists and pictures of animals beginning with the same letter and make them into their own alphabet book. Use the story as a starting point.

Surprise!

Many stories have a twist at the end to surprise readers or make them laugh. You could look for other examples to share, or make up your own.

Animal stories

Many traditional folktales feature animal characters, such as Anancy and Brer Rabbit. Look for them in libraries and bookstores.

Reading and Writing

If you and your child have enjoyed reading this book together, you may also enjoy writing about it together. Shared writing, like shared reading, is a wonderful way to help develop children's early literacy skills. Encourage children to write or draw their own version of the story, their feelings toward the story, or an experience from their life that relates to the story in some way. You may wish to paste their work on these two pages as a keepsake and a record of their literacy development. Children not yet ready to write may enjoy dictating a story for you to write down for them. For more information and ideas about writing and reading with your child, please see the *Reading Together at Home Parents' Handbook*.

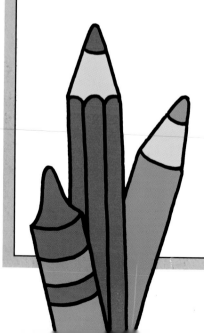

Reading Together at Home

Green Level: Taking Off

How this book helps support your child's reading development:

"Have You Seen the Crocodile?" is a wonderful book for children beginning
to read as it combines a simple, repetitive text with a satisfying story.
Children will quite quickly be able to read it independently.
The words are very spare, so children have to fill in the gaps in the story
and make their own interpretations. For instance, the ending is unclear —
has the crocodile eaten the animals or not? — and this
gives you lots to discuss with your child.
The illustrations follow the story, often telling more than the words.
Children will enjoy spotting the crocodile in the pictures
long before it is mentioned in the text.

See the *Reading Together at Home Parents' Handbook* for
more information on specific reading skills your child is developing
as he or she reads books in the Taking Off level
of the *Reading Together at Home* series.